Questions and Answers: Countries

Italy

A Question and Answer Book

by Nathan Olson

Consultant:
Susanna F. Ferlito
Department of French and Italian
University of Minnesota
Minneapolis, Minnesota

Capstone
press

Mankato, Minnesota

Fact Finders is published by Capstone Press,
151 Good Counsel Drive, P.O. Box 669, Mankato, Minnesota 56002.
www.capstonepress.com

Library of Congress Cataloging-in-Publication Data
Olson, Nathan.
  Italy: a question and answer book / by Nathan Olson.
  p. cm.—(Fact finders. Questions and answers. Countries)
  Includes bibliographical references and index.
  ISBN 0-7368-3754-X (hardcover)
  1. Italy—Juvenile literature. I. Title. II. Series.
DG417.O44 2005
945—dc22   2004011305

Summary: Describes the geography, history, economy, and culture of Italy in a question-and-answer format.

Editorial Credits
Megan Schoeneberger, editor; Kia Adams, set designer; Kate Opseth, book designer; Nancy Steers, map illustrator; Wanda Winch, photo researcher; Scott Thoms, photo editor

Photo Credits
Art Resource, NY/Scala, 6–7
Beryl Goldberg, Photographer, 12, 27
Bruce Coleman Inc./Danilo Donadoni, 17
Capstone Press, 20, 29 (bill and coins)
Corbis/Owen Franken, cover (foreground), 24–25; Tim De Waele, 19
Corel, 1, 13
David R. Frazier Photolibrary, 14–15
Getty Images Inc./AFP/Nico Casamassima, 9; Giuseppe Cacace, 20–21
John Elk III, 4, 11
Photo courtesy of Nick Ladd, 23
StockHaus Ltd., 29 (flag)
SuperStock/Steve Vidler, cover (background)

Artistic Effects
Comstock, 16; Corel, 6; Ingram Publishing, 18

1 2 3 4 5 6 10 09 08 07 06 05

Table of Contents

Features

Where is Italy?

Italy is a country in southern Europe. It is about the size of the U.S. state of Arizona.

Italy is a **peninsula**. A peninsula is a piece of land with water on three sides. Italy is shaped like a high-heeled boot. Several islands lie off Italy's coast. The two biggest islands are Sicily and Sardinia.

The peaks of the Dolomites surround many small villages and towns. ▶

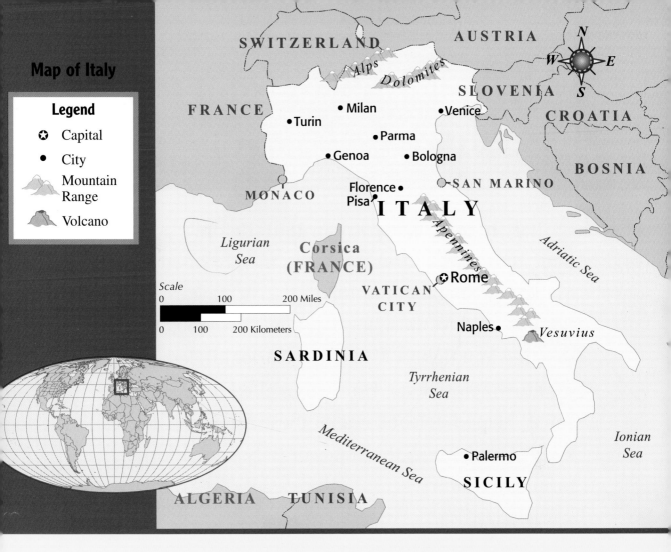

Map of Italy

Legend
- ✪ Capital
- • City
- ⛰ Mountain Range
- 🌋 Volcano

SWITZERLAND

AUSTRIA

N
W   E
S

Alps

Dolomites

SLOVENIA

FRANCE

• Milan

• Venice

CROATIA

• Turin

• Parma

BOSNIA

• Genoa

• Bologna

○ SAN MARINO

MONACO

Florence •

I T A L Y

Pisa •

Ligurian Sea

Corsica (FRANCE)

Apennines

Adriatic Sea

Scale

0   100   200 Miles

0   100   200 Kilometers

VATICAN CITY

✪ Rome

SARDINIA

Naples •

Vesuvius

Tyrrhenian Sea

Ionian Sea

Mediterranean Sea

• Palermo

SICILY

ALGERIA

TUNISIA

Mountains cover much of Italy. The Alps and the Dolomites stand in the north. The Apennines stretch down the center of the country. Some of Italy's mountains are volcanoes. Six of the volcanoes are active and sometimes erupt.

When did Italy become a country?

Italy became a country in 1861. Before then, Italy was a series of states, mostly ruled by foreign kings. In the 1830s, Italians began fighting against these foreign kings. In 1860, one freedom fighter, Giuseppe Garibaldi, led his army across Italy. His army, called the red shirts, helped defeat some of these foreign kings. One by one, the states of Italy joined to form one country.

Fact!

By 1946, Italians no longer wanted a king or queen. They voted to end the monarchy and form a republic. A year later, Italians agreed on a constitution.

Garibaldi's soldiers fought many battles for Italian unity.

On March 17, 1861, Italians named Victor Emmanuel II as the first king of Italy. But the country wasn't complete yet. Venice became part of Italy in July 1866. Rome joined the country in 1870.

What type of government does Italy have?

Italy is a parliamentary **republic**. This type of government has at least one main leader and a lawmaking group called **parliament**.

Italy has both a president and a **prime minister**. The president has the power to declare war. The president also chooses the prime minister. The prime minister runs the government and leads parliament.

Italy's parliament has two houses. The Chamber of Deputies has 630 deputies. The Senate has 315 senators.

Fact!

Italy's president must be at least 50 years old. The U.S. president can be as young as 35 years old.

Italians cast ballots to vote in elections.

Voters choose Italy's leaders. Anyone 18 years old or older may vote for the president and deputies. But voters must be 25 years old to vote for senators.

What kind of housing does Italy have?

In cities, many Italians own or rent apartments. Most apartments have balconies that overlook the streets. Colorful plants often line the balconies.

In villages, houses are built close together. They are made of wood, stone, or brick. Most houses have three or four bedrooms.

Where do people in Italy live?

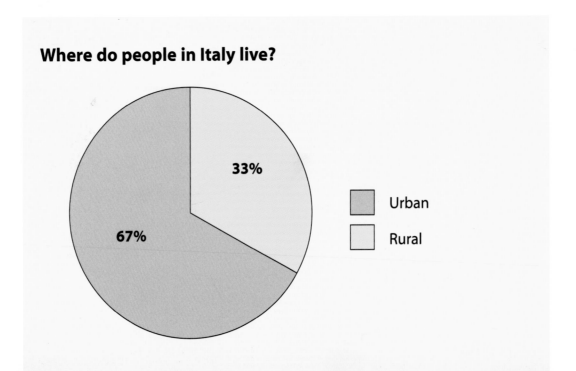

33%

67%

Urban

Rural

Colorful homes and flowers line many Italian streets.

Fewer Italians live in the countryside. Some of these people live in fancy homes called **villas**. Others live in small houses or cottages.

What are Italy's forms of transportation?

Italians drive over the country's many paved roads. Italians own cars, mopeds, and motorbikes. More than 1.6 million Italians own mopeds. Many Italians also use public transportation. Italy has more public buses than any other country in Europe.

Some riders travel through Milan on streetcars. ▶

The city of Venice has **canals** instead of roads. People travel around the city on water buses called vaporetti. They can also ride through the canals in long, thin boats called **gondolas**.

What are Italy's major industries?

Manufacturing is Italy's top **industry**. Two well-known Italian car companies are Fiat and Ferrari. Ferrari makes fast sports cars. Other Italian companies produce steel, chemicals, and computers.

Tourism is another large industry. Tourists from around the world visit Italy. They eat in restaurants, shop in stores, and enjoy Italy's many works of art.

What does Italy import and export?

Imports	Exports
metals	cars
petroleum	chemicals
textiles	food

Workers make car doors at the Fiat factory in Milan.

Farming and fishing are important to Italy. Italian farmers grow tomatoes, olives, and grapes. These foods are used to make pasta sauce, olive oil, and wine. Fishers catch swordfish, red mullet, and white shark in Italy's coastal waters.

What is school like in Italy?

Most Italian students go to school six days a week. Classes begin at 8:30 in the morning. At 12:30 in the afternoon, students go home for lunch. After lunch, they go back to school for one or two hours.

Most Italian children go to public schools. They begin elementary school when they are about 6 years old. Elementary school lasts seven years.

Fact!

Classes in Italy usually have between 10 and 25 students.

Italian grade school students work on a science lesson.

All students take a test at the end of elementary school. Students who pass the test go to secondary school for at least two years. After two years, students can choose to go on to upper secondary school.

What are Italy's favorite sports and games?

Soccer is the national sport of Italy. Italians of all ages watch and play soccer. They call the game *calcio* (KAHL-choh). Most cities have their own *calcio* team.

Italians also enjoy other sports. Italy hosts many pro ski and bicycle races each year. Formula One auto racing and basketball are also popular sports in Italy.

Fact!

Early Romans were among the first people to play bocce ball. They used coconuts brought from Africa.

Italy (in blue) played Croatia in the 2002 World Cup competition.

Bocce ball is a popular game invented in Italy. Players throw wooden balls at a smaller target ball. The first Italian league of bocce ball formed in 1947. Italy often plays in the Bocce World Championship, which has been held every year since 1947.

What are the traditional art forms in Italy?

Italy is known for its **architecture**. In Rome, visitors can see the Colosseum. This large stadium opened in AD 80. The Leaning Tower is in Pisa. This famous tower leans because it was built on soft soil.

Many famous artists worked in Italy during the **Renaissance**. Michelangelo Buonarroti painted the ceiling of the Sistine Chapel. Leonardo da Vinci painted the *Mona Lisa* and *The Last Supper*.

Fact!

Italian Antonio Stradivari made about 1,100 stringed instruments before he died in 1737. They were so well made that more than half of his instruments still exist. In 1988, one of his cellos sold for $1.2 million.

Opera is one of Italy's most popular art forms. Operas are musical plays in which performers sing their lines. Italian Giuseppe Verdi wrote 26 operas in the 1800s. Today, his operas are performed more often than operas by any other composer.

What major holidays do people in Italy celebrate?

Italians celebrate Christmas on December 25. The Christmas season continues to January 6, which is known as Epiphany. Italian children look forward to the night of January 5. Children are told that a witch known as La Befana visits homes with presents that night.

On August 15, Italians celebrate Ferragosto. Businesses close while people go to the beach or enjoy picnics.

What other holidays do people in Italy celebrate?

Carnevale
Easter
Labor Day
New Year's Day

Christmas decorations and lights hang above an Italian street.

Italians also celebrate national holidays. June 2 is Italian National Day. On this date in 1946, Italy became a republic. April 25 is called Liberation Day. On this day, Italians celebrate the end of World War II (1939–1945).

What are the traditional foods of Italy?

Pasta is Italy's most famous food. Pastas such as lasagna, tortellini, and ravioli are favorites. Some Italian families make fresh pastas and sauce each day.

Italians are famous for many other foods. In northern Italy, people eat a rice dish called risotto. The city of Parma is known for Parmesan cheese. Italians also enjoy a tasty ice cream treat called gelato.

Fact!

In Italy, lunch is often the biggest meal of the day.

A pasta maker runs sheets of dough through a machine to make fresh noodles.

Italians invented pizza. In 1773, an Italian cook in Naples, Italy, opened the first pizza shop. He cooked the pizza in a brick oven heated with lava. The lava came from the volcano Mount Vesuvius near the city.

What is family life like in Italy?

Italians sometimes call children the royalty of Italy. Parents take pride in their children. Many Italian children are named after saints. Some young adults live with their parents until they are 30 years old.

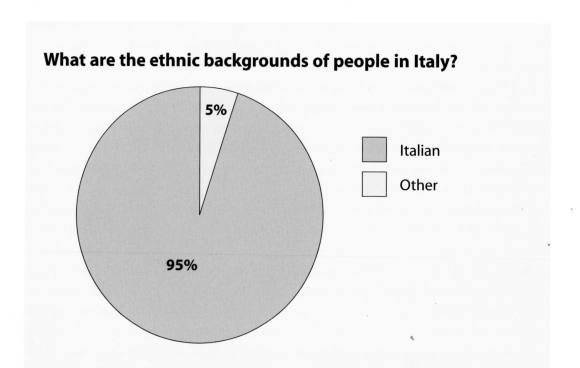

What are the ethnic backgrounds of people in Italy?

5%

95%

Italian

Other

A family walks through the streets of Gubbio in central Italy.

Today, many Italian families have only one child. In the past, families were very large. The mother was in charge of caring for the family, cooking meals, and cleaning the house. Today, many women work outside the home. Grandparents help care for children.

Italy Fast Facts

Official name:

Italian Republic

Land area:

*113,521 square miles
(294,019 square kilometers)*

**Average annual
precipitation (Rome):**

31.6 inches (80.3 centimeters)

**Average January
temperature (Rome):**

*46 degrees Fahrenheit
(8 degrees Celsius)*

**Average July
temperature (Rome):**

*74 degrees Fahrenheit
(23 degrees Celsius)*

Population:

57,998,353 people

Capital city:

Rome

Language:

Italian

Natural resources:

marble, natural gas, petroleum

Religions:

*Roman Catholic   95%
Other   5%*

Money and Flag

Money:

Italy's money is the euro. In 2004, 1 U.S. dollar equaled 0.82 euro. One Canadian dollar equaled 0.61 euro.

Flag:

The Italian flag has green, white, and red stripes. During the late 1700s, people designed the flag to look like the French flag. They used green instead of blue for the first stripe. Italy kept the same flag when it became a republic in 1946.

Learn to Speak Italian

Most people in Italy speak Italian. It is Italy's official language. Learn to speak some Italian using the words below.

English	Italian	Pronunciation
good-bye	arrivederci	(ah-ree-vuh-dur-CHEE)
hello or good-bye	ciao	(CHOW)
yes	si	(SEE)
no	no	(NOH)
please	per favor	(PER fah-VOH-ray)
thank you	grazie	(GRAH-zee-uh)

Glossary

architecture (AR-ki-tek-chur)—the planning and designing of buildings

bocce ball (BAH-chee BAWL)—a game similar to lawn bowling where players throw wooden balls at a smaller target ball

canal (kuh-NAL)—a channel through which water flows

gondola (GON-duh-luh)—a light boat with high, pointed ends, used on the canals of Venice, Italy

industry (IN-duh-stree)—a single branch of business or trade

parliament (PAR-luh-muhnt)—the group of people who have been elected to make laws in some countries

peninsula (puh-NIN-suh-luh)—a piece of land that is surrounded by water on three sides

prime minister (PRIME MIN-uh-stur)—the leader of a parliament, a government body that makes laws

Renaissance (REN-uh-sahnss)—the period of art and learning in Europe in the 1400s and 1500s

republic (ree-PUHB-lik)—a government headed by a president with officials elected by the people

villa (VIL-uh)—a large, fancy house, especially one in the country

Internet Sites

FactHound offers a safe, fun way to find Internet sites related to this book. All of the sites on FactHound have been researched by our staff.

Here's how:
1. Visit *www.facthound.com*
2. Type in this special code **073683754X** for age-appropriate sites. Or enter a search word related to this book for a more general search.
3. Click on the **Fetch It** button.

FactHound will fetch the best sites for you!

Read More

Britton, Kathryn. *Italy.* The Changing Face of. Austin, Texas: Raintree Steck-Vaughn, 2003.

De Capua, Sarah. *Italy.* First Reports. Minneapolis: Compass Point Books, 2003.

Malone, Margaret Gay. *Italy.* Discovering Cultures. Tarrytown, N.Y.: Benchmark Books, 2003.

Index